Edith Nesbit

The Railway Children

Edith Nesbit

鐵路少年

Illustrated by Zosia Dzierzawska

The Commercial Press ELI

Contents 目錄

故事錄音開始和結束的標記

start ▶ stop ■

Main Characters

Mother
Peter
The old gentleman

Before you read

Grammar

1 Read a part of an email. Complete the email with the verbs below.

are	changes	enjoy	~~have~~	is	leave	live

I'm reading *The Railway Children* at school. Edith Nesbit wrote this book in 1906. Do you *have* to read this book at your school? It's about three children. Their names are Bobbie, Peter and Phyllis. They (**1**) .... in London with their mother and father. But one day, everything (**2**) .... They (**3**) .... London with their mother. At first, the children are sad to leave their home. They don't know that their new house (**4**) .... near a railway station. In 1905, trains (**5**) .... exciting. And railway stations are interesting places. 100 years ago children didn't travel on trains very often. And so the children in the story (**6**) .... themselves. And this is why they become the Railway Children.

2a Here is how the story begins. Cross out the incorrect word.

They ~~*wasn't*~~*/weren't* always the Railway Children. At first they were just Bobbie, Peter and Phyllis; three children who lived in a big house (**1**) *at/in* London. They didn't get the train very often. And they (**2**) *didn't/doesn't* know much about the railway then. Bobbie was 14 years old. She was a kind girl, and she always tried to help (**3**) *people/persons*. Then there was Peter. One day, he wanted (**4**) *being/to be* a train driver. And Phyllis (**5**) *was/were* 8 years old, and very curious.

2b **Now read the first paragraph of the story on page 8 and check your answers.**

3a **Read this conversation between Bobbie and Peter and put the words into the contracted form.**

Bobbie: 'Are you playing with your train?'
Peter: 'No, I am *I'm* not. (**1**) I am .... really sad. Look!'
Bobbie: '(**2**) Do not .... worry. Father is coming home soon. (**3**) He will .... help you.'
Peter: 'I can hear Father now. (**4**) He is .... here. But I (**5**) cannot .... ask him to help me now. (**6**) I will .... ask him when he finishes his dinner.
Bobbie: Yes, (**7**) that is .... the best thing to do.

3b **Why is Peter sad about his train? Look at the picture on page 11 to find out.**

4 **Match the description to a place in the story.**

the bedroom	the dining room	the garden
the kitchen	~~the railway~~	the railway station

Where you can find the trains and the station. ....*the railway*........

1 This is where you cook. ....
2 This is where you sleep. ....
3 You go here to get a train. ....
4 There are a lot of flowers here. ....
5 This is where you eat dinner. ....

Chapter 1

A New Home

▶ 2 They weren't always the Railway Children. At first they were just Bobbie, Peter and Phyllis; three children who lived in a big house in London. They didn't get the train very often. And they didn't know much about the railway then. Bobbie was 14 years old. She was a kind girl, and she always tried to help people. Then there was Peter. One day, he wanted to be a train driver. And Phyllis was 8 years old, and very curious[1].

The children lived in a beautiful house, with their mother and father. Mother was always there. She helped them with their school work. And she read them stories. Father did an important job for his country. He had a lot to do. But after work, he always had time to play with the children.

Bobbie, Peter and Phyllis were very happy. So, how did these children become the Railway Children? Well, now I'm going to tell you.

We'll begin our story on a very important day.

1. curious: 好奇

It was Peter's birthday. He was ten years old. And he had a very nice party. There was a lot of good food, and nice games to play. But what Peter really wanted was a toy[1] train for his birthday. And that is what he got. It was a beautiful train. And he played with it all day. In the evening, Bobbie went into Peter's bedroom. She wanted to say happy birthday again.

'Are you playing with your train?' she asked.

'No, look! It's broken[2].' Peter tried not to cry[3]. 'I'm a big boy now. And big boys don't cry,' he thought.

'Don't worry,' said Bobbie. 'Father is coming home now for dinner. He'll help you.'

At dinner, Peter waited. 'I can't ask my father now', he thought 'I'll wait, and I'll ask him when he finishes his dinner. But please finish dinner soon!' When the family finished eating, Peter couldn't wait another minute. 'Father, look at my train! What can I do?'

'Don't worry Peter', said Father. 'We'll look at it together.'

1. toy: 玩具 ▶KET◀
2. broken: 壞了 ▶KET◀
3. to cry: 哭泣 ▶KET◀

'We!' said Peter.

'Yes, me, you, Bobbie and Phyllis,' said Father.

'But they're girls!' said Peter.

'Girls are clever too you know,' said Father.

At that moment, there was a knock[1] at the door. 'Who can that be?' said Father. 'It's very late. Stay in the dining room children.' Mother and Father went to open the door. And the children waited in the dining room. They were very curious.

'Who is it?' asked Bobbie. 'It's strange[2]. People don't usually come to visit in the evening.'

'I'm going to listen,' said Phyllis. And so, Phyllis went near the door and tried to listen. She couldn't hear everything. 'There are two men with Father. They're in the kitchen. Father is talking,' said Phyllis. 'He's not happy. I can hear more now… They're going outside. Yes, that's it, now the men are leaving. I don't know if Father is with them. Yes, they're leaving.'

Phyllis went back to the table, but only Mother came back into the dining room.

'Go to bed now children,' said Mother. 'It's late.'

'But what about my train?' said Peter.

1. a knock: 敲門　　**2. strange:** 奇怪 ▶KET◀

'Father isn't here,' said Mother. 'He had to go to work.'

'That's strange,' said Bobbie. 'Why does Father have to go to work now? It's late'. The children said goodnight to their mother, and they went to bed.

The next morning, the children were ready for their breakfast. But they didn't have breakfast with Mother or Father. They weren't there. But their Aunt Emma was in the kitchen.

'First, Father isn't here. And now Mother. What's happening?' thought Phyllis. 'Aunt Emma is here. And she doesn't tell us stories. She doesn't help us with our school work. She's got no time for children.' Mother didn't come home all day. The children went to school. But when they came back, there was only Aunt Emma. In the evening, Mother came home. She sat down, and then she said: 'Now my dear children, I want to tell you something. It's bad news[1]. Father will not be home for a long time. I'm very worried about this. So, you must help me. You must be good. Please don't ask me any questions. Don't worry. Everything will be fine in the end.'

1. news: 消息 ▶KET◀

In their bedroom, the children couldn't sleep. 'What's happening? Bobbie, can you speak to Mother?' asked Peter.

'No! We mustn't ask questions. And Mother must have a good reason[1] for not telling us. We promised[2] to be good, remember? It's something about father's job. We have to wait. We can't do anything now.'

After that, Mother often went out. And Aunt Emma stayed with the children. One evening, Mother came home late. She was very tired.

'Now my children,' said Mother. 'We're leaving this house. We're going to live in a new house. It's called "Three Chimneys". You'll love it. I know.'

'Everything is changing,' thought Bobbie. 'What's going to happen next?'

'Can I take my toy train?' asked Peter.

'Yes,' said Mother. 'But we can't take everything with us. "Three Chimneys" is small.'

The children were worried. Where was this new house? And how small was it?

One week later, they were on the train to begin their new life. At first, the children enjoyed

1. reason: 原因 ▶KET◀ **2. promised:** 答應

looking out of the train window. But soon they were tired.

After many hours, the train arrived. They got off the train and looked around[1]. They couldn't see very much. They were cold, tired and hungry. And it was very dark. 'We have to walk now,' said Mother. And so they walked. They saw a lot of farms. And then, they saw a hill.[2]

'Where is the house?' asked Peter.

'It's up this hill,' said Mother.

And so, they went up the hill. And then they saw a house. 'Look! There it is,' said Mother.

They opened the door. It was very dark and cold inside. Mother had a candle[3], and so they began to see more and more.

'I can see some things now,' said Phyllis. 'There's a table… and I can see some chairs. But there's not much in the room. There's a place for a fire[4]. But there's no coal[5]. That's why it's very cold.'

'What's that noise?' asked Bobbie.

'It's only a rat[6],' said Mother.

'A rat!' said the children, all together.

1. **looked around:** 四處張望
2. **hill:** 山 ▶KET◀
3. **candle:** 蠟燭
4. **fire:** 爐火 ▶KET◀
5. **coal:** 煤塊
6. **rat:** 老鼠

After-reading Activities

Reading

1 Read these sentences about the house in London and "Three Chimneys" and underline the right word.

The old house was in London/*near the railway.*

1 The house in London was *big/small*.

2 Peter had a birthday party in the *old house/new house*.

3 Some men visited Father in the *old house/new house*.

4 "Three Chimneys" was *big/small*.

5 "Three Chimneys" was *warm/cold*.

6 "Three Chimneys" *was dark/wasn't dark*.

Writing

2a Put the words in the correct order to make questions.

a Is Father Where? *Where is Father?*

b is Father coming back When? When ....

c at work Father Why is? Why ....

d you playing your train with Are? Are ....

e is house new Where the? Where ....

f take Can toy train I my? Can ....

2b Now match the answers to the right questions.

1 It's near a railway station. ....

2 I don't know. ....

3 No, it's broken. ....

4 Yes, but you can't take too many things. ....

5 He has a lot of things to do. ....

6 He's at work. *a*

Grammar

3 Put the words in the box in the plural form to complete the sentences.

chair	farm	~~friend~~	person	story	question

Her name was Roberta, but *friends* called her Bobbie.

1 Mother always told the children ....
2 After dinner some .... visited Father.
3 When Father left, the children wanted to ask Mother some ....
4 Near the railway station there were many ....
5 In the new house Phyllis could see a table and some ....

4 Complete the sentences. Put the verbs in brackets in the past tense.

There (be) *was* a knock at the door. The children (**1**) (wait) .... in the dining room. They (**2**) (be) .... very curious. Some men (**3**) (go) .... into the kitchen. Father (**4**) (talk) .... to them. He (**5**) (not be) .... very happy. Phyllis (**6**) (listen) .... near the door. Then the men (**7**) (leave) .... with Father.

Before-reading Activity

Listening

4 **5a Listen to track 4 of Chapter 2. What can't the children eat?**

1 ☐ bread and jam
2 ☐ bread with jam and butter
3 ☐ bread with butter

5b Why does Mother say this? Read the next chapter to find out.

Chapter 2

Peter's Idea[1]

▶ 3 'Wake up!' said Bobbie. 'We're in a new house, remember?'

'Yes, a new house with a rat,' said Phyllis.

'But, it's exciting,' said Peter. 'I want to go outside. We didn't see much last night. It was too dark.'

'Yes, I want to go out,' said Bobbie. And so, they went into the garden.

'It's very green,' said Phyllis.

'That hill,' said Bobbie. 'We didn't like it last night. We had to go up with our bags. It's better to go down a hill.' And so, they ran down the hill.

'Wait! I can see the railway track,[2] and a tunnel[3]', said Peter. 'I want to go there.'

They started running again. And soon they arrived at the track.

'It's fantastic,' said Bobbie. And then they heard a noise. It was from the tunnel.

Choo choo, Choo choo!

1. idea: 主意 ▶KET◀
2. track: 路軌
3. tunnel: 隧道

It was a train. And it was very fast.

'That was exciting,' said Peter.

'Yes it was,' said Phyllis. 'To be very near a train, and to see all of it. Often at the station you can't see all of the train at the same time. I want to go to the station now.'

'Good idea!' said Bobbie. They followed[1] the track, and soon they arrived. 'We usually go to the station to get a train. Or to meet someone. But today we are here because we want to be here. And it's only us. No Mother, and no Father.'

The station was an exciting place. There were many things to do.

At home there were also many things to do. They helped to cook and clean the house. 'No more rats,' said Bobbie. The children were happy. The house, the hill, and the station were new and very interesting.

But in June it started raining. The children couldn't go out. And the house was cold.

'Mother,' said Peter, 'can we have a fire?'

'No dear,' said Mother. 'We haven't got much

1. followed: 沿着 ▶KET◀

coal. Coal is expensive. Go and play. Then you'll be warm again.'

▶ 4 At dinner-time, the children looked at the table. There was bread and butter and jam.

'You can have jam or butter on your bread. Not jam and butter. We don't have a lot of money,' said Mother.

▶ 5 No jam and butter, and no coal. This is really bad,' Peter thought. 'At the station there's a lot of coal.' Then he had an idea.

After dinner, Peter called his sisters. 'I've got an idea,' he said. 'Come with me to the station. And bring some bags with you.'

'Alright,' said Bobbie and Phyllis.

When they arrived, Peter put some coal in his bag. 'Quick! Help me!' he said to his sisters.

'But stealing[1] is wrong,' said Bobbie. 'We mustn't do this.'

'We need to do it Bobbie. We need some coal. We're not stealing. There's so much coal here. They don't need it all.'

'Alright,' said Bobby. 'But we have to be quick.'

1. stealing: 偷竊 ▶KET◀

But then they heard a noise. 'There you are!' It was the porter[1]. 'I've got you now, you bad children' he said. 'We're not bad,' said Peter. The porter had a candle, and he looked at the children.

'Well, you're the children from "Three Chimneys". Why did you do this? Don't you know it's wrong to steal?'

'I didn't think it was wrong,' said Peter. 'There was so much coal. You didn't need it all. We had no coal for a fire. We were cold, Mother was cold and...'

'Well,' said the porter. 'We'll forget about this. But remember young man: it's wrong to take something that's not yours. Don't do it again.'

'I won't steal anything again. Thank you so much,' said Peter. 'We'll go home now.'

The children tried to stay at home. But it was difficult. It was very interesting at the station. And very different from life in London. Soon, they decided to go back.

'We'll only watch the trains. We won't do anything bad again,' said Bobbie.

1. porter: 行李員

They went to the station every day. And they learnt all the times of the trains that arrived. The porter's name was Perks. He saw the children every day. 'I was wrong about those children,' thought Perks. 'They're good. And they're really interested in the trains.'

One morning the children were near the tunnel. 'Maybe the next train is going where Father lives now. I really want to see him again,' said Phyllis.

'Me too,' said Peter. 'The 9.15 train is arriving now. We can wave[1] at the passengers.' The train went by, and the children started to wave. On this train there was an old gentleman[2]. He had white hair, and he wore a large hat. And from a train window the children saw a hand. This hand held[3] a newspaper. It was the old gentleman's hand.

From that day at 9.15 the children waved at the train. The old gentleman always waved at them. 'Maybe the old gentleman knows Father. And he'll tell him that we wave every day,' thought Bobbie.

1. wave: 揮手
2. gentleman: 紳士
3. held: 拿着 ▶KET◀

The children asked Perks a lot of things. And Perks tried to answer all their questions. They were now good friends. Every day the children went to the station. They stayed with Perks. And they waited for the 9.15 train.

But one day, they couldn't wave at the train. Mother wasn't well. She had to stay in bed. 'I'll be better when I rest,' said Mother. But in the evening, she didn't feel better.

'I'm going to get the doctor,' said Bobbie. 'He'll help Mother.' Soon the doctor arrived.

'What is it? What's wrong?' asked Bobbie.

'She needs some medicine[1],' said the doctor. 'The house must be warm. And she needs some good hot food and a lot of tea.'

'Mmm, all things that are very expensive,' thought Bobbie. 'We don't have the money. What can we do? Think Bobbie. Think!'

That evening, the children took a sheet from their bed.

What did they do with the sheet? Well, soon you'll know.

1. medicine: 藥物 ▶KET◀

Reading

1 Number these sentences in the order that they happen in Chapter 2.

- **a** ☐ The children wave at the 9.15 train.
- **b** ☐ *1* The children wake up.
- **c** ☐ The porter sees the children taking the coal.
- **d** ☐ An old man waves at the children.
- **e** ☐ The children go to see the tunnel.
- **f** ☐ Mother doesn't feel very well.
- **g** ☐ The children go to the station.
- **h** ☐ The children take some coal from the station.

2 Read the sentences and cross out the incorrect word.

Bobbie wanted to go down the hill ~~*so*~~*/because* it was easy.

1. In June the children wanted to go out *but/so* it started raining.
2. There was no coal for a fire *because/so* Peter wanted to get some from the station.
3. The children liked the station *because/but* it was an interesting place.
4. Mother didn't feel well *but/so* Bobbie went to get the doctor.
5. The children asked the porter many questions *because/but* they were curious.
6. The children took a sheet from the bed *because/but* we don't know why.

Vocabulary

3 Make some expressions from Chapter 2. Match a word from column A to a word from column B.

	A		B
1	[d] hot	a	hill
2	[ ] dinner	b	children
3	[ ] green	c	window
4	[ ] bad	d	~~food~~
5	[ ] train	e	station
6	[ ] railway	f	time

Grammar

4 Read some questions that the children ask Perks. Put the right word in the gap.

How	How many	When	Where	~~Why~~

Why do trains have numbers?

1 .... old is the train driver?
2 .... does the 9.15 train arrive in London?
3 .... people get the train every day?
4 .... is the next station?

Before-reading Activity

Listening

▶ 6 **5 Why do the children need the sheet? Listen to the first part of Chapter 3 and tick (✓) the right answer.**

1 [ ] To clean the train window.
2 [ ] To sleep at the station.
3 [ ] To tell the old gentleman something.
4 [ ] To play a game.

Chapter 3

The Old Gentleman

▶ 6 At 9.15 the next morning, the old gentleman was on the train. He stopped reading his newspaper. 'Here's the tunnel. We're near the station,' he thought. 'I'll wave at those three nice children again.'

The train came out of the tunnel. And he looked out of the window. But he didn't see three children. He only saw one. It was Peter. And Peter had a sheet in his hands. And there were some words on the sheet. It said:

LOOK OUT OF THE WINDOW! AT THE STATION!

▶ 7 The train stopped at the station. And the old gentleman looked out of the window. Then he saw Phyllis, running to his window. 'I thought, … I was late,' she said. And then she gave the old gentleman a letter. Soon the train started again and he read the letter.

Dear Mr…We don't know your name,
Mother is ill. And we have to buy some medicine. But we don't have much money. Can you help us? Father isn't here and we don't know his address. Father will pay you when we see him. Here are the things that Mother needs.
Thank you so much.

The old man looked at the letter again. And then he smiled[1].

That evening at 6.00 a big box arrived at "Three Chimneys". The children opened the box. And inside there was some medicine – and some other things they needed. And there was a letter to the children.

Dear Children,
Here's the medicine. Tell your mother it's from a friend. She'll be better soon. Don't worry.

1. smiled: 微笑

And the old gentleman was right. Two weeks later, the children made another sheet. On this sheet they wrote.

SHE'S BETTER. THANK YOU FOR THE MEDICINE!

When the old man saw it, he smiled and waved at the children again.

The train passed and then Peter said, 'Now we have to tell Mother about the old gentleman.' The children went home. And they told Mother everything. But Mother wasn't very happy.

'You mustn't talk to others about our life. Will you promise this?'

The children promised. They were very sorry.

But soon they were happy again. The next day was Bobbie's birthday. On the table there were many good things to eat, and a birthday cake. Bobbie was very happy. At the end of the party, Peter gave his sister something.

'It's the toy train,' said Peter. 'I know it's my train. But now it's also your train. We can play with it together.'

'Thank you Peter,' said Bobbie. 'You're a good brother. This is a really great day. Thank you everybody.' The next day, Bobbie looked at the train. 'It's beautiful,' she thought. 'Peter is really sad because it's broken. But I know what I'll do.'

One hour later Bobbie was at the station. She waited for the next train. And when it arrived she got on.

'Excuse me! Driver! Driver! Can you help me?' she said. But the driver couldn't hear her. 'Please driver, I've got my brother's toy train and it's broken and...'

But then the train left the station. 'Help me!' said Bobbie. 'Stop the train!' But still the driver couldn't hear Bobbie. Then the driver saw something. There was a little girl. And she was very frightened.

'What are you doing here?' said the driver. 'You can't stay here. It's dangerous[1].'

'I'm sorry,' said Bobbie. 'I've got this toy train. It's my brother's and it's broken. Can you help me? It's really important.' The driver looked at the toy train. And then he looked at Bobbie.

1. dangerous: 危險 ▶KET◀

'She's only a little girl,' he thought. 'Well,' said the driver, 'I could try. I have a friend. Maybe he can help me. But first we have to take you home.' And so, at the next station Bobbie got off the train. The driver helped her to get another train. A train for her town. 'Well, Bobbie,' said the driver, 'I know where you live. I'll try to help you with your brother's toy train.'

'What an interesting day! Now I can do something nice for my brother,' she thought.

And two days later her brother had a very big surprise[1]. 'Peter, come to the station with me,' said Bobbie.

'Why?' asked Peter.

'Because I want you to meet someone. It's... a surprise.' said Bobbie.

And so, Bobbie and Peter went to the station. At the station there was a man on the platform.[2]

'Hello Peter,' said the man. 'I'm a train driver. I know you want to be a train driver one day. Your sister told me. I have something for you.' And then the driver gave Peter his toy train.

1. surprise: 驚喜 ▶KET◀ **2. platform:** 月台 ▶KET◀

Peter took the train. 'I can't believe it. A real train driver. And my train, it's new again' said Peter. 'Thank you.'

◈◈◈

One day, the children were at the station again. They had to meet their mother. 'When is Mother arriving?' asked Phyllis.

'Very soon,' said Bobbie. 'We'll wait here. She'll be tired, and we can help carry her bags.' Then the children heard a strange noise.

'What is it?' asked Peter. There were a lot of people on the platform. The children could hear Perks.

'OK everybody,' said Perks. 'Please stay back[1]. I need to do my job.' And then the children heard another man. It wasn't English. But what language was it?

'I want to see what's happening,' said Bobbie. 'We can help.' The children went near the group of people. And they saw a man. He had grey hair, and his clothes were dirty.

1. stay back: 站在原地不要動

'I can speak a little French,' said Peter. 'I learnt it at school. I can speak to him.'

'OK' said Perks. 'I don't think he's French. But maybe he understands that language.'

'Parlez-vous français?[1]' asked Peter. The man stopped speaking. And then he started speaking again. But this time he spoke very quickly. 'Er…he speaks French,' said Peter. 'But I don't understand.'

'Don't worry,' said Bobbie. 'Mother will be here soon. Take him to your room Perks. And we'll wait for her. Mother can speak French well. And she's on the next train.' And so they waited. When Mother arrived, she went to the room. And then she started speaking to the man. They spoke for a long time. And the children watched and waited.

'Well, Mother, who is he?' asked Peter.

'He's Russian,' said Mother. 'And he can't find his ticket. I'll take him home with us. Don't worry. He's a nice man. He writes books – beautiful books. I know some of them. I read one the other day. He needs to rest, and to be warm. I'll tell you some more about him tomorrow.'

1. Parlez-vous français?: 你會說法語嗎？

After-reading Activities

Reading

1 Read the sentences and put the names of the people in the gaps.

Bobbie	Mother	~~Peter~~	Phyllis
The Russian man	the train driver		

...*Peter*... had a sheet in his hands.

1 .... gave the old gentleman a letter.
2 Peter gave .... a part of his toy train.
3 Bobbie went to the station to speak to ....
4 .... couldn't speak English.
5 .... spoke to the Russian man when she arrived at the station.

Grammar

2 Read the sentences and underline the right preposition.

The old man was *at/on* the train.
1 The old gentleman looked *out of/to* the window.
2 There were some words *in/on* the sheet.
3 The train stopped *at/to* the station.
4 The old gentleman saw Phyllis run *at/to* his window.
5 The old gentleman read a letter *from/to* the children.
6 The old gentleman looked *at/to* the letter again and smiled.

Vocabulary

3 Look at these words and circle the odd one out.

	a	bedroom	**b**	a kitchen	**c**	(a garden)	**d**	a dining room
1	**a**	a tunnel	**b**	a platform	**c**	a track	**d**	a hill
2	**a**	medicine	**b**	bread	**c**	butter	**d**	jam
3	**a**	French	**b**	London	**c**	English	**d**	Russian
4	**a**	hat	**b**	a coat	**c**	a shirt	**d**	a sheet
5	**a**	mother	**b**	porter	**c**	driver	**d**	doctor

Writing

4 Complete another letter that the children wrote to the old gentleman.

better	can	friend	medicine	speak	wave	~~writing~~

Dear Mr, ...
We are *writing* to say thank you for the (**1**) ....
Mother is (**2**) .... thanks to you. Mother says that we mustn't (**3**) .... to others about our life. But we know that we (**4**) .... speak to you.
You're our (**5**) .... We'll see you tomorrow when we (**6**) .... at the 9.15 train.
The Railway Children

Before-reading Activity

Listening

▶ 9 **5a Listen to track 9. One statement is false. Which one is it?**

1 ☐ The weather is really bad.
2 ☐ A tree is on the track.
3 ☐ The children are on the track.

5b Now look at the picture on page 41 to see if you are right.

Chapter 4

Stop the Train!

8 The next day, the children woke up early. They wanted to know more about the strange man. 'Mother, what happened to him?' asked Phyllis.

'Yes, please tell us,' asked Bobbie.

And so, Mother told them. 'Well, you know he's a writer. He wrote a beautiful book about poor people – and how to help them. And in Russia he went to prison[1] for it. Sometimes people go to prison for the wrong reason. He was in prison for three years. When he left, he wanted to find his family. But he couldn't find them. He left Russia. And now he's looking for his family here.'

'Oh that's very sad,' said Bobbie.

'Yes it is,' said Mother. 'Just think. He wasn't guilty[2] of anything.'

9 The next day, the Russian man was better. The children stayed at home for three days. They wanted to help him. But, after three days, they

1. prison: 監獄 2. guilty: 有罪

also wanted something else. They really wanted to go to the railway again.

'We can go and find some fruit for him. That will be a nice surprise,' said Bobbie.

'Yes,' said Peter. 'There's lots of fruit near the tunnel.' And so, they went down the hill. When they were near the tunnel, Peter was very happy. 'We can watch the trains and we can work at the same time,' he said. Then the children heard a noise. It was a very big tree.

'Look! Look at that tree! It's going to fall,' said Bobbie. And then the tree fell on the track. 'Oh no!' said Bobbie. 'This is very dangerous. A train is coming soon. And the tree, it's on the track.'

'What can we do?' asked Peter. 'The 11.29 train will arrive soon. We have to go to the station to tell somebody.'

'There's no time,' said Bobbie. 'It's 11.00.'

10 'We need something red,' said Peter. 'Then we can use it to wave at the train before it arrives here. Phyllis, Bobbie, our coats are red. We can use them.'

'Good idea!' said Bobbie and Phyllis.

The children waited at the other end of the tunnel. Soon they heard a noise. 'It's coming! It's coming,' said Peter.

The children waved their coats at the train.

'The driver won't see us,' said Bobbie. The train was near and it was fast. 'It's not stopping,' said Bobbie. 'I'm going to stand on the track. Then the driver will see me.'

'No Bobbie! It's too dangerous,' said Phyllis. But it was too late. Bobbie was on the track.

'Stop, stop, stop!' said Bobbie. The train was very close now. And then, slowly the train stopped. Just in front of poor Bobbie. The driver got off the train. And Peter and Phyllis ran to the driver to tell him about the tree.

'There's a tree…on the track. At the other end of the tunnel,' said Peter.

'Well, if it's true you three children are heroes[1]' said the driver. 'But what about the girl, on the track?' Bobbie was still there. She was very frightened. 'We have to take her home, poor girl!'

1. heroes: 英雄

Soon everybody knew about the tree on the track. The children went back to the station. And everybody smiled and waved at them. They were not just the railway children now. They were the heroes from "Three Chimneys." Some days later, a letter arrived.

Dear Sir and Ladies,
We want to thank you. And the people on that train want to thank you. You children are heroes. We're having a party for you at three o' clock on the 30th of this month.

The children wrote a letter.

Thank you very much. We were very happy to help. It's very nice of you to have a party for us. We'll be there!

The children washed their best clothes. And they waited for the day.

'I'm very excited,' said Peter.

'Me too,' said Phyllis.

The day arrived and they went to the party. It was at the station. There were flowers, a lot of food, and a lot of people. Many people came to thank the children.

'I was on that train,' said one man. 'Thank you!'

'You are heroes,' said another man. But the children looked for one special[1] person. And there he was! The old gentleman from the 9.15 train. He stood in front of the people. And then he started to speak.

'I'd like to give something to these special children,' he said. 'They did a great thing. Bobbie, Peter and Phyllis. You're the heroes from "Three Chimneys". And we're all very happy to know you.' And then he gave each of the children a watch – a beautiful gold watch.

'Peter, say something,' said Bobbie.

'Er… You're very kind,' said Peter. 'It was nothing really. And it was very exciting. Well, what I want to say is… er… Thank you very much.'

It was a great party. The children enjoyed every

1. special: 特别的 KET

minute of this special day. They were ready to go home. But then Bobbie had an idea. She spoke to the old gentleman.

'I want to ask you something,' she said. And then Bobbie told him about the Russian man. 'Where are his wife and children? He's very sad. Maybe you can find some information to help him. You're so clever.'

'What's his name?' asked the old gentleman. Bobbie wrote the name on a piece of paper.

S-Z-E-Z-C-P-A-N-S-K-Y

The old man looked at the name. 'That name,' he said. 'I... know one of his books. I read it two or three years ago. I'm very happy you asked me about him. I know many Russians in London. And every Russian knows his name. I'll try to get some information. And now tell me about you.' And then Bobbie told the old gentleman about London and about "Three Chimneys", and about many other things.

Ten days later the children heard a knock at the door. It was the old gentleman. 'Hello,' he said. 'I have some good news. I know where the Russian man's wife and children are. Can I speak to him?'

'Yes, yes, that's great[1]. I'm so happy,' said Bobbie. The children were very curious. And so they waited and watched. They watched the old gentleman speaking to the Russian. And then they saw the Russian man put his hands on his face. At first he cried. But then he smiled. And he smiled for a long time.

'Well,' said Bobbie. 'I'm so happy that his story has a happy ending.'

1. that's great: 那真好

Reading

1 Number these sentences in the order that they happen.

a ☐ The train stopped in front of Bobbie.
b [1] The children heard a noise.
c ☐ The tree fell on the track.
d ☐ The children heard the train.
e ☐ The children waved at the train with their coats.
f ☐ Bobbie went on the track.

2 Read these sentences and decide who is speaking.

Bobbie	Mother	The Old Gentleman
Peter	~~Phyllis~~	The train driver

'Mother, what happened to the Russian man?' *Phyllis*
1 'There are people who are in prison for the wrong reasons.' ....
2 'Look! Look at that tree! It's going to fall.' ....
3 'You three children are heroes.' ....
4 'I'd like to give something to these special children.' ....
5 'We need something red.' ....

Vocabulary

3 What food and drink is at the party? Unjumble the words.

keac *cake*
1 tiurf ....
2 eta ....
3 dwesasnich ....
4 eewsts ....
5 eesche ....
6 rdaeb ....

Spelling

4 'What's his name?' asked the old gentleman. Bobbie wrote the name on a piece of paper.

S • Z • E • Z • C • P • A • N • S • K • Y

Can you spell the Russian man's name? Try to spell it and then listen to the CD to see if you are right.

Before-reading Activity

Listening

▶ 11 **5a Listen to the first part of Chapter 5. Who is Mother speaking to? Tick the right answer.**

1 ☐ Phyllis
2 ☐ Peter
3 ☐ Bobbie

5b What is Mother worried about? Tick the right answer.

1 ☐ Father will never come home.
2 ☐ Peter and Phyllis don't remember their father.
3 ☐ Peter and Phyllis don't speak to her.
4 ☐ Father did something wrong.
5 ☐ Bobbie is ill.

Chapter 5

The Big Secret[1]

▶ 11 One day, Bobbie made some tea for her mother. 'Thank you,' said Mother. 'Bobbie, do you think that Peter and Phyllis are forgetting their father?'

'No!' said Bobbie. 'Why?'

'Because they don't speak about him now,' said Mother.

'We speak about him when you're not here. When you're at home, we don't say anything. We don't want you to be sad,' said Bobbie.

'Bobbie,' said Mother. 'Something bad happened to us… to Father… when we left London. It's true. I'm very sad when I think of it. But you must never, never forget him.'

'Oh no, Mother, I won't,' said Bobbie.

'Good,' said Mother. 'Your father will come home soon. Please don't speak to your brother and sister about our conversation.'

'I won't say anything, I promise,' said Bobbie. ■

1. secret: 秘密

▶ 12 That evening Mother told the children a story. She told them about their father when he was young. The story was very funny, and the children enjoyed it. 'We must help Mother,' thought Bobbie. 'We mustn't ask too many questions because she gets sad. But where is Father? Where can he be?' Bobbie was very worried. But soon, she had something different to think about.

The next day, Peter was ill. The doctor came to "Three Chimneys". Peter had to stay in bed for a week. One week for a ten-year-old boy is a very long time. Peter didn't know what to do. Bobbie was sad for her brother. 'Is there anything I can do?' she thought. 'He can't go out. But I can. I'll go to the station and find some newspapers for him to read.' And so Bobbie went to the station.

'Hello Bobbie,' said Perks. 'How are you?'

'I'm fine,' said Bobbie. 'But Peter isn't very well. Do you have any newspapers I can take home? '

'Yes, I'll get some,' said Perks. 'People always leave them on the train.' And so ten minutes later, Bobbie walked home. She had lots of newspapers.

And she had to carry them up the hill. She looked at the newspapers. They were really heavy. But she was happy to help her brother. And then she saw something.

'No! What's this?' she thought. 'It can't be him. But it is! And then she started to read. 'So now I know,' she thought.

What did Bobbie read? And why was it so bad? These were some of the words she read:

PRISON – FIVE YEARS – GUILTY

And next to these words was a picture of… her father! 'I must try not to tell anybody. Not even Mother,' thought Bobbie.

When Bobbie got home, Mother was in the kitchen.

'What is it?' said Mother. 'I know something is wrong[1]. Your face is red.'

'Nothing,' said Bobbie. 'I'm tired.' Bobbie went to her bedroom. She put the newspaper under her bed. Soon it was time for dinner. The children sat at the table with their mother. They did this every day. But something was different today. Usually, Bobbie

1. something is wrong: 出現問題

News
GUILTY!
5 years
in prison

spoke a lot. But today she didn't say anything. After dinner, Mother spoke to Bobbie again.

'There's something wrong! Why aren't you speaking? Why are you sad? What is it? Tell me now!' Bobbie didn't say anything. She just took the newspaper from under her bed, and gave it to her mother.

And now all Bobbie could say was, 'Read! Read!' And so Bobbie's mother read the newspaper.

'Oh Bobbie,' said Mother. 'Do you believe it? You don't, do you?'

'NO!' said Bobbie.

'Good!' said Mother. 'Because it's not true. Your Father is in prison. But he didn't do anything wrong. He's not guilty. He's a good man. Are you going to tell the others?' asked Bobbie's mother.

'No,' said Bobbie. 'We mustn't tell anybody. It'll be our secret.'

'That's right,' said Mother. 'And now I'm going to tell you everything. Bobbie sat on her bed and listened to the story. 'The men who came to our house that night… the last time you saw Father.

top secret

They were policemen. They wanted your Father. They asked about some letters. These letters were in Father's office. … The letters had secrets in them… secrets that another country wanted. The policemen said this to your Father:

"You are stealing secrets. And you gave some letters to the Russians. It's true, you're guilty. We found some more letters in your desk."'

'That's impossible![1]' said Bobbie. 'Father loves his country.'

'Somebody did it,' said Mother. 'And the letters were in Father's desk. Someone put the letters there. Someone didn't like Father. And that is the guilty person.'

'Who was it? Who could do this?' asked Bobbie.

'There was a man and he didn't like your father. He wanted Father's job. And now, he's got it. Your father is very clever. This man didn't like him for this reason.'

'Can't we tell somebody about this?'

'Nobody will listen,' said Mother.

'Well, I know a man, a very special man. He will listen,' thought Bobbie.

1. That's impossible!: 絕不可能！

That night, Bobbie wrote a letter. She gave the letter and the newspaper to Perks at the station.

My dear friend,
Please read the newspaper. There is some news about my Father. It's not true. Father never did it. He isn't guilty. Mother says it was another man. This man didn't like Father. And this man now has Father's job. You're very clever. You found the Russian man's family. Can you help us again?
Peter and Phyllis don't know anything.
Please help us.
Bobbie

Who was the letter for? Well, I think you know. It was for an old gentleman. An old gentleman, who was always on the 9.15 train.

It was difficult. It was very difficult. But Bobbie didn't tell Peter and Phyllis about Father. 'I'll just wait,' thought Bobbie. 'My dear friend will help us. I know he will.'

Reading

1 Read the sentences and underline the right answer.

Mother told the children a story about *their father*/*London*.

1 *Peter/Phyllis* was ill.
2 Bobbie went to the station to get some *sweets/newspapers*.
3 Bobbie spoke to *Perks/the Old Gentleman* at the station.
4 Before they had dinner, Bobbie *told Mother everything/didn't tell Mother anything*.
5 Father was in prison for stealing *money/secrets*.
6 Bobbie wrote a letter to *Perks/the Old Gentleman*.

2 What does Mother believe? Choose the right answer.

1 ☐ Father is guilty. He is coming home in five years.
2 ☐ Nobody is guilty. Father is coming home soon.
3 ☐ Another man is guilty of stealing the secrets.

Grammar

3 Choose the correct title for the newspaper article.

1 ☐ A man will to go to prison for five years.
2 ☐ A man will go to prison for five years.
3 ☐ A man going to prison for five years.
4 ☐ A man go to prison for five years.

Writing

4 Re-write the sentences below.

	The job of Father.	*Father's job*
1	The birthday of Peter.	....
2	The toy train of my brother.	....
3	The hand of the Old Gentleman.	....
4	The family of the Russian man.	....
5	The desk of Father.	....
6	The bed of Bobbie.	....
7	The friend of Bobbie.	....

Before-reading Activity

Listening

▶ 13 **5a Listen to the first part of Chapter 6. Where are the children? Choose the right answer.**

1 ☐ At the station
2 ☐ On the hill
3 ☐ In the tunnel

5b Listen again. What do you think the children will do next?

1 ☐ They'll go into the tunnel.
2 ☐ They'll wait on the hill.
3 ☐ They'll go to the station to ask for help.

Chapter 6

Home Again

▶ 13 One day, the children were on the hill. 'Look!' said Phyllis. You can see the tunnel from here.' And then Phyllis saw another thing. 'Can you see those boys, near the tunnel? They're running. They're running into the tunnel. How many are there? One–Two–Three–Four–Five–Six. Six boys.'

'I'm going to the other part of the hill,' said Peter. 'I want to watch them come out.'

'We want to come too,' said Phyllis and Bobbie.

The three children went to the other part of the hill. After five minutes the boys came out. And Phyllis counted again. 'One–Two–Three–Four–Five. Five! But where is number six? He's not coming out.' ■

▶ 14 They didn't sit on the hill for long. They went into the tunnel to look for the boy. When you are on a train, a tunnel is exciting. And this was a very long tunnel. But walking in a tunnel is not exciting. It's dark, it's dangerous, and there are rats[1].

'Can't we go to the station, to ask for help?' said Phyllis. 'I don't like it in here.'

'No, we have to look here now,' said Bobbie. 'We don't have much time.' They looked everywhere. They had a candle. But it was very dark. And then they saw something. It was a boy. The children ran to him.

'Is he sleeping?' asked Phyllis.

'I don't know,' said Peter.

'Speak to us! Say something! Wake up!' said Peter.

At that moment, the boy woke up. 'Who are you?' he asked.

'We're from "Three Chimneys," said Bobbie. 'We're here to help.'

'My leg. I can't walk,' said the boy.

'Try!' said Peter.

'I can't,' said the boy. 'I have to sit down.'

'I'll stay with him,' said Bobbie. 'I have the candle. You go to find someone who can help. But

1. rats: 老鼠

be quick! Before a train comes. Remember, we only have one candle.'

Peter and Phyllis left. And Bobbie and the boy were alone[1].

'My name's Jim. Thank you for helping me. You're a hero.'

'That's OK,' said Bobbie.

Peter and Phyllis came out of the tunnel. 'That wasn't easy,' said Peter. 'We have to find some help.' Phyllis looked around.

'Look!' said Phyllis. 'I can see a farm.'

'Good! Run now,' said Peter. And so they ran. And soon they arrived at a house. They knocked on the door. And they heard a noise. There were people inside the house. Together with Peter and Phyllis, they went into the tunnel to get Bobbie and Jim. Then they took Jim to "Three Chimneys."

Mother was very surprised. 'Mother!' said Bobbie. 'We have a boy. We found him in the tunnel.'

'I'll get the doctor,' said Mother. The doctor arrived, and the children waited.

1. **alone:** 獨自一人 KET

'He'll be fine,' said the doctor. 'But he needs to rest[1]. He must stay here for three weeks. And he mustn't go out.'

Peter was happy. 'It'll be nice to have another boy in the house,' he thought.

The next day there was a knock at the door.

'That will be the doctor,' said Mother. 'I'll go. You wait here children.' The children waited. And they listened. It was a man. But it wasn't the doctor.

'I know that voice,' said Phyllis.

'Children, come here,' said Mother. 'It's Jim's grandfather.' The children went to meet the man. And who was this man? Well, it was the old gentleman, from the 9.15 train. Their friend. It was a great surprise to see him again.

'Is Jim going home now?' asked Peter.

'No, he needs to stay here. Your Mother is very kind. You'll all help Jim to get better.'

Soon the old gentleman had to leave. 'Bobbie will you walk with me to the station?' he asked.

1. rest: 休息 ▶KET◀

Bobbie and the old man went down the hill. 'I read your letter,' said the old man. 'I'm trying to understand what happened to your father. Don't worry I'll have some news soon.'

'He didn't do anything bad,' said Bobbie.

'I know that,' said the old gentleman.

Jim soon got better. He was a nice boy. Everybody liked him. But the children were sad. They wanted to see Father again.

'Something good will happen, I know it,' said Phyllis. And Phyllis was right. Something very good happened.

The next morning the children woke up early. 'Do you know,' said Phyllis, 'that we never wave at the 9.15 train now?'

'You're right,' said Bobbie. 'We could go this morning if you want.'

'Yes, good idea[1]!' said Peter and Phyllis. Soon they were near the tunnel, ready to wave. The train went by. And the old gentleman waved. That was normal. He always did that. But this time something was different. Everybody on the train

1. good idea: 好主意

waved. And all of them had a newspaper in their hand.

'Well,' said Bobbie.

'Well,' said Peter.

'Well,' said Phyllis. 'What does this mean?' The children didn't know. They had to go home. They had their school work to do. But Bobbie couldn't read or write anything. She thought about the train.

'Mother, can I go for a walk[1]? I don't want to study today. I want to be alone.' Bobbie went into the garden. But she couldn't stay there. Something was strange. And she had to go to the station now. When she arrived, she saw Perks. 'Hello Perks,' she said.

'Hello Bobbie,' said Perks. He had a newspaper in his hand too.

'Why does everybody have a newspaper?' thought Bobbie.

'I'm very happy for you on this important day,' said Perks.

'Why is it important?' asked Bobbie.

1. **go for a walk:** 散步

'But, don't you know?' asked Perks. 'It's in the newspaper.'

'What's in the newspaper?' asked Bobbie.

At that moment the 11.54 train arrived. And Perks went to the platform.

'What's happening today?' thought Bobbie.

Only three people got off the 11.54 train. On the platform there was a young woman. And there was a young man. And the other person was… Well, you know, don't you?

'Oh daddy, my daddy,' was all you could hear. And all you could see was a tall slim man[1], with a little girl in his arms.

'I knew it, I knew it,' said Bobbie.

Bobbie and her father went home. 'Did your Mother read my letter? Did she read the newspaper?'

'No, she doesn't know anything,' said Bobbie.

'Go inside the house alone.' said Father. 'Tell her that I'm home. That other man did those bad things. It wasn't me. This is all thanks to the Old Gentleman, on the 9.15 train.' Bobbie went inside.

1. a tall slim man: 又高又瘦的男人

And Father waited. And then, after five minutes he knocked on the door. To come back home; to the family he loved very much.

After-reading Activities

Reading

1 Choose the correct option.

How many boys came out of the tunnel?
a ☑ five **b** ☐ six

1 Who stays with Jim in the tunnel?
a ☐ Bobbie **b** ☐ Peter

2 Where do the children find somebody to help them?
a ☐ at the station **b** ☐ at a farm

3 How long does Jim have to stay at "Three Chimneys"?
a ☐ two weeks **b** ☐ three weeks

4 Who is Jim's grandfather?
a ☐ the Old Gentleman **b** ☐ Perks

5 Why didn't Bobbie want to study?
a ☐ because she was tired **b** ☐ because something was strange.

6 What is different about the 9.15 train?
a ☐ only the old gentleman waves **b** ☐ everybody waves

Writing

2 Read the conversation and put in the right word.

coming	go	~~know~~	told	was	worked

Man: 'Did you ...*know*... the father of the Railway Children is not guilty?'
Woman: 'Yes, a friend (**1**) .... me this morning.'
Man: 'The children will be happy.'
Woman: 'Yes, you're right. Who (**2**) .... guilty then?'
Man: 'It was another man. He (**3**) .... with the Railway Children's father.'
Man: 'Oh, so now he'll (**4**) .... to prison.'
Woman: 'Yes, and the father is (**5**) .... home today.'

Grammar

3 Read the questions that the children ask their father. Match the questions to the answers.

1 [e] Are we going back to London now?
2 [ ] What did you eat in prison?
3 [ ] Did you meet the Old Gentleman?
4 [ ] Were you sad in prison?
5 [ ] Where was the prison?
6 [ ] Did you write to Mother?

a Yes I spoke to him. He's very nice.
b Yes, I wrote to her every day.
c It was in London, near our old house.
d Yes I was. I couldn't see my beautiful children.
~~e~~ I don't know. We have to decide.
f I ate bread and some vegetables most of the time.

4a Put the words in the box into the right category. Use the table below.

bedroom	bread	dining room	excited		
flowers	garden	happy	hill	jam	kitchen
sad	platform	station	tea	track	tunnel

Feelings	Food and Drinks	House	Nature	The Railway
....	....	....	....	....
....	....	....	....	....
....	....	....	....	....
....	....	....	....	....
....	....	....	....	....

4b Now add two more words you know to each category.

Edith Nesbit

Her Early Life

Life was difficult for Edith Nesbit when she was a child. Her father died when she was only four years old. She lived in Surrey, near London. Her sister was often ill. So the family had to change houses often to find places with good weather. For this reason, it was not easy for Edith to go to school. She was never in one place for a long time. So she usually studied at home and read a lot of books. When she was seventeen, her family finally moved to London. And when she was nineteen, she met her husband. Her husband's name was Hubert Bland, and he was a writer.

Her Work

Edith Nesbit started writing when she was young. She wrote poems to get money for her family. Then she wrote books like *The Prophet's Mantle* (1885) and *The Marden Mystery* (1896). Not many people read these books. And so, in 1899, Edith began writing books for children. And it was because of these books that she became famous. Many children read her books. Some of them were *The Adventures of the Treasure Seekers* (1899), *Five Children and It* (1902), and of course, *The Railway Children* (1906).

The Railway Children

Edith Nesbit will always be famous for *The Railway Children*. Children still read this book today. People see it as a very modern children's story. The story also teaches us many things about life in the early 1900s. And we can learn many things about the railway in these times.

Did You Know?

- There are two *Railway Children* films. One in 1970 and another thirty years later, in the year 2000.
  When Edith Nesbit wrote about Bobbie, she often thought about a friend. Her name was Berta Ruck.

- There is a group called *The Railway Children* which helps children who don't have a home.

Focus on...

Southend On Sea is about 50 miles from London

The Train in the early 1900s

Phyllis: *To be so near a train, and to see all of it. Usually, at the station you can't see all of the train; at the same time. I want to go to the station now. What do you think?*

A train journey in the 1900s was something important and exciting for children. This is why the Railway Children always want to go to the station or near the tunnel. They have a lot of fun there.

Children at this time didn't often go on the train. A train was something different and new. Many people in these times didn't have enough money for a holiday. Children in London, for example, sometimes went to the sea for a day. This is called a day trip. They went to towns like Southend on Sea. And they travelled there by train

Waiting for the train

The train journey was part of the fun. Families went to the station. They waited on the platform. There were always many people, and a lot of noise. Children bought their sandwiches and waited there to begin their journey.

On the Train

When they got on the train, the journey was quite long. The train often stopped at different stations. The trains were slow. But for the children of these times, they were fast. Eight people could sit in each part of the train. Children often looked out of the window. They wanted to be the first to see the sea. When they arrived, porters helped to carry people's bags. Then the families could enjoy their relaxing day trip on the beach.

The Steam Train

The first trains used steam engines. Look at the picture. You can see one of these trains. A man called Thomas Newcomen made the first steam engine. Then another man, James Watt, made these trains faster. Steam engines also helped to move boats. Big boats, called ships, also used steam engines. The famous ship, 'The Titanic' used steam as well. Steam engines used coal. But this was very dirty, and it was not very safe. That is why many trains now use electricity and not steam.

1 Underline the words that Bobbie, Peter and Phyllis use to describe the train.

clean <u>dangerous</u> dirty fast exciting new
noisy old quiet safe

2 What words do you use to describe trains today. Are they different?

Girls playing hopscotch

Children playing ring-a-roses

Children in the early 1900s

What was life like for children in the early 1900s? They certainly didn't have television, internet, smart phones, and other things like that. They did other things to have fun. And life in the family, at school and at work was very different.

Games

Peter loved his toy train. But there were other things that children used to have fun. Children often played a game called 'marbles'. Marbles are small balls, made of glass. They were different colours. Children played with their marbles in the streets. Another game was 'hopscotch'. Children jumped onto the numbers that you can see in the picture. They jumped onto numbers 1, 4 and 7 on one leg. And they jumped onto numbers 2 and 7, 5 and 6, and 8 and 9 on two legs.

Home

The family was very important at this time. Children had to do what their mother and father told them to do. Many people thought that boys were better than girls. The most important thing for boys was to find a job. For girls it was important to find a husband. That is why *The Railway Children*, is called the first modern story for children. Do you remember what Father said to Peter in Chapter 1? 'Girls are clever too.' Father wanted Bobbie and Phyllis to help with Peter's train. This was a strange idea at this time.

School

When the Railway Children went to live at "Three Chimneys" their mother was their teacher. In London they went to school. School at this time was free for all children under 12. To go to school after this age was very expensive. When children were 13 they often went to work. Rich children went to schools that cost a lot of money.

Boys playing marbles

Work

Life was difficult for children in this period. The Railway Children didn't have to work. But many children worked at a very early age. Children could go to school until they were 12. But many children didn't go to school. They worked because their family needed the money. At 13 all children could work. A poor child could clean the houses of rich people, or he could sell things on the street. But many children worked in factories.

In the book you often see the words 'Mother' and 'Father' with a capital 'M' and a capital 'F'. Why do you think Edith Nesbit does this?

1 ☐ Because capital letters are always used with these words.
2 ☐ Because it shows that they are very important to the children.
3 ☐ Because it shows that they are very old.

Test Yourself 自測

Choose the correct person for each question. Bobbie (B), Peter (P) Phyllis (Ph).

		B	P	PH
	Who has a toy train and wants to be a train driver one day?	☐	☑	☐
1	Who listens to Father speaking to the two men who come to the house in London?	☐	☐	☐
2	Who decides to take some coal from the station?	☐	☐	☐
3	Who decides to take a sheet from the bed to tell the old gentleman something?	☐	☐	☐
4	Who asks a train driver to look at the toy train?	☐	☐	☐
5	Who tries to speak French to the Russian man?	☐	☐	☐
6	Who stands on the track to stop the train?	☐	☐	☐
7	Who reads the newspaper that speaks about Father?	☐	☐	☐
8	Who sees the boys going into the tunnel?	☐	☐	☐
9	Who stays with Jim in the tunnel?	☐	☐	☐
10	Who sees Father on the platform?	☐	☐	☐

Syllabus 語法重點和學習主題

Topics
Love
Feelings
Family
Trains
Nature

Grammar and Structures
Simple Present: states and habits
Present Continuous: actions in progress
Past Simple: finished actions
Future forms: Present Continuous, going to, will
Can: ability, permission
Could: ability, permission in the past
Must: obligation
Have to: necessity
Will: offers, spontaneous decisions for future, predictions

Adjectives
Prepositions (place, time)
Pronouns
Question Words
Relative Clauses
There is/There are
Verbs + infinitive/ing

Answer Key 答案

The Railway Children

Pages 6-7

1 **1** live **2** changes **3** leave **4** is **5** are **6** enjoy
2a **1** in **2** didn't **3** people **4** to be **5** was
2b check your answers.
3a **1** I'm **2** Don't **3** He'll **4** He's **5** can't **6** I'll **7** that's
3b look at the picture to find out
4 **1** the kitchen **2** the bedroom **3** the railway station **4** the garden **5** the dining room

Pages 16-17

1 **1** big **2** old house **3** old house **4** small **5** cold **6** was dark
2a **a** Where is Father? **b** When is Father coming back? **c** Why is Father at work?
d Are you playing with your train? **e** Where is the new house? **f** Can I take my toy train?
2b **1** e **2** b **3** d **4** f **5** c **6** a
3 **1** stories **2** people **3** questions **4** farms **5** chairs
4 **1** waited **2** were **3** went **4** talked **5** wasn't **6** listened **7** left
5a 2
5b Read the next chapter to find out.

Pages 26-27

1 b - e - g - h - c - a - d - f
2 **1** but **2** so **3** because **4** so **5** because **6** but
3 **1** d, **2** f, **3** a, **4** b, **5** e, **6** b
4 **1** How, **2** When, **3** How many, **4** Where
5 3

Pages 36-37

1 **1** Phyllis **2** Bobbie **3** the train driver **4** The Russian man **5** Mother
2 **1** out of **2** on **3** at **4** to **5** from **6** at
3 **1** a hill **2** medicine **3** London **4** a sheet **5** mother
4 **1** medicine **2** better **3** speak **4** can **5** friend **6** wave
5a 1

Pages 46-47

1 b - c - d - e - f - a
2 **1** Mother **2** Bobbie **3** The train driver **4** The Old Gentleman **5** Peter
3 **1** fruit **2** tea **3** sandwich **4** sweets **5** cheese **6** bread
4 Student's Own Answer
5a Bobbie
5b 2

Pages 56-57

1 **1** Peter **2** newspapers **3** Perks **4** didn't tell Mother anything **5** secrets **6** the Old Gentleman
2 3
3 2
4 **1** Peter's birthday **2** My brother's toy train **3** The Old Gentleman's hand **4** The Russian Man's family **5** Father's desk **6** Bobbie's bed **7** Bobbie's friend
5a 2
5b a – They'll go into the tunnel.

Pages 68-69

1 **1** a **2** b **3** b **4** a **5** b **6** b
2 **1** told **2** was **3** worked **4** go **5** coming
3 **1** e **2** f **3** a **4** d **5** c **6** b
4a **Feelings:** excited, happy, sad
Food and Drinks: bread, jam, tea
House: bedroom, dining room, kitchen
Nature: flowers, garden, hill
The Railway: platform, station, track, tunnel
4b Student's Own Answer

Page 73

1 Fast, exciting, noisy
2 Student's Own Answer

Page 75

2

Page 76

1 **1** Ph **2** P **3** B, P & Ph **4** B **5** P **6** B **7** B **8** Ph **9** B **10** B

Read for Pleasure: *The Railway Children* 鐵路少年

作　　者：Edith Nesbit
改　　寫：Michael Lacey Freeman
繪　　畫：Zosia Dzierzawska
照　　片：Shutterstock
責任編輯：黃家麗
封面設計：丁　意
出　　版：商務印書館（香港）有限公司
香港筲箕灣耀興道 3 號東滙廣場 8 樓
http://www.commercialpress.com.hk
發　　行：香港聯合書刊物流有限公司
香港新界大埔汀麗路 36 號中華商務印刷大廈 3 字樓
印　　刷：中華商務彩色印刷有限公司
香港新界大埔汀麗路 36 號中華商務印刷大廈 14 字樓
版　　次：2017年 12 月第 1 版第 1 次印刷

ISBN 978 962 07 0467 3
Printed in Hong Kong